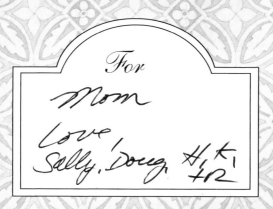

For

Mom

Love,
Sally, Doug, Hi, Ki,
+ R

DEAR MOM

With Love

Compiled by Esther L. Beilenson

Design by Lesley Ehlers

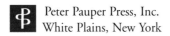

Peter Pauper Press, Inc.
White Plains, New York

For my Mom

Copyright © 1996
Peter Pauper Press, Inc.
202 Mamaroneck Avenue
White Plains, NY 10601
All rights reserved
ISBN 0-88088-113-5
Printed in Singapore
7 6 5 4 3 2 1

Contents

INTRODUCTION

Every mother remembers the first time she told her child that she loved him or her. It was on the day the baby was born. On that special day, a mother prays that her child will grow up healthy and have a future full of joy and success.

When a woman becomes a mother, her entire life changes and her personality is altered. Her child's needs come before her own. She becomes fiercely protective, wanting always to ensure the child's well-being.

A mother's love is reflected in every aspect of her child's development. And when the child, if a daughter, has children of her own, the mother's acts of kindness and concern are repeated in the actions of the daughter. It is in this sense that every generation of women sees a part of their mothers in themselves—and is happy to find it.

We hope that you will find the letters and quotations in *Dear Mom* entertaining, inspiring, and thought-provoking, and that you will discover some of your mother/your child/yourself in these pages.

E.L.B.

Motherhood

Dear Mom,

Well, it happened just as you said it would. All of the pain and doubt were completely worth it. My baby is the most beautiful baby I have ever seen. I know, I know, all mothers say the same thing about their children, but that doesn't mean it isn't true.

I get the most profound pleasure just watching my daughter. Her tiny feet, her tiny fingers, her whole little body are so cute that she looks like a little angel. Did you have this reaction with me?

The situation still isn't real to me. I guess that once I have to get up for a few more 3:00 A.M. feedings reality will set in. Somehow, I think I should be more exhausted than I am. Yesterday she made the funniest face while I was feeding her. She's all gurgles and coos once she's fed. It may sound obsessive, but I've already taken several rolls of film of her.

Even though I felt that my life was complete before, I can now tell that it was a beautiful but empty package. My friends, my career, my possessions, the life that I was so worried about disturbing, were nothing. I would do anything for my daughter, even exchange my life for hers. When she's grown I'll go back to doing what I did before. Right now, I want to be with her every waking moment and even some half-asleep. I want to thank you for convincing me that I could have it all, if I wanted it.

Love,
Christine

Motherhood has been the most joyous and important experience of my life. I would die for my children.

Carly Simon

❖❖❖

The drama of birth is over. The cord is cut, the first cry heard: a new life has begun . . . The mother—seeing, hearing, perhaps touching her baby—scarcely notices the world suddenly busying itself around her, let alone how much her body aches. She just participated in a miracle.

Carrol Dunham

❖❖❖

More than in any other human relationship, overwhelmingly more, motherhood means being instantly interruptible, responsive, responsible.

Tillie Olsen

I also find that motherhood connects you to other women, creates an instant common interest. I tend to be absorbed in my own obsessions; motherhood breaks me free.

Jane Seymour

❖❖❖

There's a time when you have to explain to your children why they're born, and it's a marvelous thing if you know the reason by then.

Hazel Scott

❖❖❖

It's just a science project until suddenly there's a person. [But now] you have no idea how you'd ever live without this child.

Meg Ryan

❖❖❖

Mothers have to tell themselves that they mustn't feel guilty about anything. We can't compare ourselves to the unattainable perfection of imaginary parents.

Tammy Grimes

❍❍❍

Once motherhood begins, life becomes a lot more hectic.

Anonymous

❍❍❍

Every woman should have a child. The sense of loss must be painful for those without a maternal relationship. There's nothing more warm and sensitive than a child. You complete the full range of emotions. For me, that's what living is about.

Donna Karan

14

Women who are mothers carry a terrible weight. Every mother I know, including myself when I was rearing children, suffers from this sense of the "right way" to be a mother and having to be everything to a child.

Kathie Carlson

❖❖❖

Oh what a power is motherhood, possessing a potent spell.

Euripides

❖❖❖

Mother love is so powerful and primitive that it feels . . . "like the doctor forgot to cut the umbilical cord."

Anonymous

Boy, when you're aching for your children, that little smell, that little touch at night, mmmmm, it makes Mama so lonely.

Tanya Tucker

◊◊◊

I'd never put my husband ahead of my personal integrity. But if I had to, I'd lie, steal, and cheat on behalf of my child.

Anonymous

◊◊◊

I must say that having children does really shed a different light on things. First of all, you have to stop putting yourself as number one, because you're not anymore. Somebody else is for a while.

Annie Lennox

◊◊◊

The fun of being a parent is watching your child unfold and develop, and letting her surprise you.

Perri Klass, M.D.

❖ ❖ ❖

Our mothers are our most direct connection to our history and our gender. The void their absence creates in our lives is never completely filled again.

Hope Edelman

❖ ❖ ❖

Nobody said giving birth is easy, but there's no other way to get the job done.

Ivana Trump

❖ ❖ ❖

Motherhood is not light, optional and free of ambivalence; it is a dark, compelling force that overrides many human preferences.

Erica Jong

I don't think in terms of genetic makeup. I've always seen children as being far more mysterious than that. . . . I'm much more interested in the soul.

Jessica Lange

❀❀❀

Any time I saw somebody with a baby I started salivating. I just knew I was ready.

Michelle Pfeiffer

❀❀❀

I'm not going to get involved because Caroline is the one who will wear it [the bridal dress]. I want her to be the happiest girl in the world.

Jackie Kennedy Onassis

❀❀❀

[Did having children save you?] Yes.

Jessica Lange

❊❊❊

How eagerly we await the first inspiration! The mother, forgetful of weariness and suffering, lifts her pale face from the pillow, and listens with her whole soul. The physician, profoundly penetrated with the mystery of birth, bends in suspense over the little being hovering on the threshold of a new existence—for one moment they await the issue—life or death! The feeble cry is the token of victory—the mother's face lights up with ineffable joy, as she sinks back exhausted, and the sentiment of sympathy, of reverence, thrills through the physician's heart.

Elizabeth Blackwell, M.D.,
first female doctor of medicine in U.S.

❊❊❊

Motherhood is, in fact, never really learned. It evolves.

Sheila Kitzinger

✿✿✿

It's agony and ecstasy. There's no question that the mother-daughter relationship is the most complex on earth. It's even more complicated than the man-woman thing.

Naomi Judd

✿✿✿

. . . Singing the same traditional lullaby every night, firmly saying no to an obstinate two-year-old or teaching a six-year-old prayers. We hear the unforgettable echoes of our mother's voice in our own.

Elizabeth Fishel

✿✿✿

To be a good mother means to lose your child to the world. My mother's child has returned. I am old enough to allow her to renew our original bond, my original role in life. I am old enough to truly treasure having a mother.

Deborah Shouse

❀ ❀ ❀

As you grow older, the years in between seem to get smaller and smaller. It's not like a parent and a child anymore. The gap closes, and it becomes a friendship.

Julianne Phillips

❀ ❀ ❀

I learned . . . so much more from my mother. I always sang to my children because she sang to me. I've found that I've become my mother more and more, that I've been lucky to have had such a fascinating woman raise me.

Carly Simon

So many of the stories that I write, that we all write, are my mother's stories. Only recently did I fully realize this: that through years of listening to my mother's stories of her life, I have absorbed not only the stories themselves, but something of the manner in which she spoke, something of the urgency that involves the knowledge that her stories–like her life–must be recorded.

Alice Walker

✿✿✿

Who fed me from her gentle breast
And hushed me in her arms to rest,
And on my cheek sweet kisses prest?
    My mother.

When sleep forsook my open eye,
Who was it sung sweet lullaby
And rocked me that I should not cry?
    My mother. . . .

Ann Taylor,
My Mother

It's happening. I'm starting to sound like my mother. I guess it's inevitable. We are, after all, little computers, and whatever data's put in, is what we become. I'm starting to hear myself say the same things to my children my mother said to me: Pick it up; clean up; use your napkin; you're gonna poke somebody's eye out with that thing. Go to sleep. Wait till your father comes home . . . all those things that are so clichéd. But, it happens.

Kathie Lee Gifford

❀ ❀ ❀

Encouragement

25 December 1854

Dear Mother,

Into your Christmas stocking I have put my "first-born," knowing that you will accept it with all its faults (for grandmothers are always kind), and look upon it merely as an earnest of what I may yet do; for, with so much to cheer me on, I hope to pass in time from fairies and fables to men and realities.

Whatever beauty or poetry is to be found in my little book is owing to your interest in and encouragement of all my efforts from the first to the last; and if ever I do anything to be proud of, my greatest happiness will be that I can thank you for that, as I may do for all the good there is in me; and I shall be content to write if it gives you pleasure . . .

I am ever your ever loving daughter,
Louy
(from Louisa May Alcott to her Mother)

I'd wake up every morning, and my mother would tell me I was beautiful. I'd go to sleep every night, and my mother would tell me I was beautiful.

Felicia Gordon

◦ ◦ ◦

Even when I was a little baby, my mom let me pick out my own clothes. She'd hold up two pairs of shorts, and I'd choose the ones I liked. She wanted me to have a certain amount of respect for myself, you know.

Felicia Gordon

◦ ◦ ◦

I always told my kids that failure is not an ugly word, it's just something that didn't work. I encouraged them to try something three or four times before they decided to give up.

Daphne Gray

A mother has to give her daughter her wings by giving her the self-confidence to make decisions.

Priscilla Presley

∘ ∘ ∘

Motherhood cannot finally be delegated. Breast-feeding may succumb to the bottle; cuddling and pediatric visits may also be done by fathers, but when a child needs a mother to talk to, nobody else but a mother will do. . . . The power of being a mother is actually quite awesome when you think about it.

Erica Jong

∘ ∘ ∘

A mother is not a person to lean on but a person to make leaning unnecessary.

Dorothy Canfield Fisher

∘ ∘ ∘

She urged me to speak clearly and have a strong point of view. Then she listened to my opinion. This gave me an incredible sense of self-esteem and a feeling that what I said mattered.

Leeza Gibbons

⬥ ⬥ ⬥

There were nine kids in my family. My mother instilled in us at a very young age that you're going to be somebody, be something. She worked hard—two and three jobs. I've worked since I was 11 years old.

Shirley A. DeLibero

⬥ ⬥ ⬥

Children thirst to hear where they came from . . . they need to know that they were desired, that their birth was a wonder, and that they were always the object of love and care.

Marcelle Clements

My mom's a survivor and that's what she gave me. She's my only role model.

Carrie Fisher

◦ ◦ ◦

Mother had a lot of courage and determination to help me achieve my dreams.

Heather Whitestone

◦ ◦ ◦

I'm just a normal mom who's really proud of them, and would love to go on and on about them.

Kathie Lee Gifford

◦ ◦ ◦

Anything good about myself I have to attribute to her. She was always very encouraging, and she trusted me with myself.

Carrie Fisher

Love

Dear Mom:

Thank you for the lovely note congratulating us on our wedding anniversary.

So much of what is good in my marriage comes from growing up in a home filled with love. You taught me to value family, and to cherish those near and dear even when their habits were so annoying.

As a teenager I must have tested your patience, thinking I knew it all. But you understood that I had to make my own decisions, and you allowed me the space necessary to grow and develop into the person I am today.

How can I thank you for all the love and support you gave and still give me? It has instilled in me the self-confidence to love all my family as they are.

Your ever-loving daughter,
Lucy

Beyond all lessons, beyond the model she provided, my mother gave me a parent's ultimate gift: She made me feel lovable and good. She paid attention; she listened; she remembered what I said. She did not think me perfect, but she accepted me, without qualification.

Fredelle Maynard

○ ○ ○

Having a baby is like falling in love again, both with your husband and your child.

Jane Seymour

○ ○ ○

It's about recognition: that mothering is hard
and important work; that mothering is more than
getting the right food on the plate or making sure
your children put on their sweaters or don't pick
their noses. Mother's Day makes us stop and
remember the hands that lay a cool washcloth on
our foreheads, that lifted us from the ground, that
held onto the back of the bicycle until we were
ready to take off on our own. It's a day for saying,
thank you Mom, for loving me that much, for
being at the bus stop, for cheering when I broke
that record, for laughing at my jokes.

Amy Oscar

○ ○ ○

My mother was not just an interesting person,
she was interested.

Joyce Maynard

○ ○ ○

Once upon a time, that all-consuming, you-are-my-everything, I'd-die-for-you feeling was our ultimate definition of love. That isn't—let us be honest here—the way most women feel about their husbands, at least not after the first five weeks of marriage. But it turns out to be how all of the women I spoke with say they feel about their kids.

Judith Viorst

∘∘∘

She always wanted my sister and me to look like we just walked out of Pierre Deux. Very French little dresses. I was a little ballerina, like a little princess. I loved it. I loved my childhood and I loved my mom.

Natasha Gregson Wagner,
of her mother, Natalie Wood

∘∘∘

She's having this love affair with this little creature who is having a love affair with her.

Mercedes Ruehl,
of Michelle Pfeiffer
and her adopted daughter, Claudia Rose

○ ○ ○

Wynonna had her head on my right shoulder, and Ashley had her head on my left. I just felt this moment of exquisite completion. They are truly my other halves, the flesh of my flesh, the bone of my bone.

Naomi Judd

○ ○ ○

I thought my mom's whole purpose was to be my mom. That's how she made me feel.

Natasha Gregson Wagner

○ ○ ○

The connection is such that these mothers may find their eyes full of tears when their children are weeping, their hearts—when their children are happy—bursting with joy.

Judith Viorst

○ ○ ○

I love my mother and I'm forever grateful for the sacrifices she made for me.

Spoken by Hope Steadman on the
TV program thirtysomething

And now [my child] makes every day like Christmas. I can't wait to see him in the morning, I can't wait for him to wake up.

Kirstie Alley

○ ○ ○

Success

Dear Mom,

I just want you to know that you have been an excellent role model. Now that I'm an adult, and about to start my own family, I can appreciate how you successfully integrated all your roles.

I am awed when I look back on my childhood, and remember you going to school, while working full-time, and also making sure that home was a happy, welcome place for us. You always made time to read to me and color with me; then, later, you helped me through "new math" and teenage angst. Through you, I saw that a balance between work, play, friends, and family was essential and achievable.

How did you keep up with it all? Now, you have settled into your career and I am grown, yet your self-confidence and determination, coupled with your constant good humor and positive outlook, remain unchanged and still affect me. I know that, because of the values you instilled in me, and because I watched you succeed, I will make good choices and pursue the right opportunities. You have given me the gift of confidence, a deep belief in the powers of the self. I hope to make my life an example, as you have made yours. Thanks for showing me what it means to be a successful woman.

Love Always,
Jane

Motherhood is the greatest thing that's ever happened to me.

Christie Brinkley

⊙⊙⊙

As a young African-American woman pursuing a degree in engineering at Michigan State University in the early seventies, Mom was hindered by one obstacle after another. Her perseverance paid off, however. Not only did she graduate, but today she teaches science at Arizona State as part of the Upward Bound program—and she encourages low-income high school seniors to pursue their college degree.

Elisa Marie Scinto

⊙⊙⊙

I think being a mother is much harder work than writing.

Alice Hoffman

I don't think there's any doubt that, for me, motherhood—and particularly my relationship with my daughter—has been one of the best experiences of my life. Watching someone grow and develop—someone who shares some of your views but not all of them, who struggles to find her own independent voice and her own identity—brings up a lot of the same issues that I face.

Hillary Rodham Clinton

◌◌◌

I'll go out there and she'll tell me all about what she's doing and show me her accomplishments, and then I'll take out my wallet and show her the pictures of my kids and say, "Look at this, this is my accomplishment." And there's really nothing better in the world.

Beth Rosen

◌◌◌

I grew up with a single working mother whose job as an executive secretary kept her active and involved with people. It doesn't matter so much that she had to work to support me, though that was a definite necessity. What does matter is that it gave her a life independent of the kitchen, and it kept me aware all through my youth that work was a part of life, as much a part as eating and sleeping.

Lauren Bacall

When stars returned home after conquering New York or Hollywood, it meant they were so successful they could afford to live closer to their mothers than to their managers.

Neal Karlen

Motherhood has changed my whole attitude about a career. Now I'd be very happy living at home with my child for the rest of my life. Being a mother is the most important thing.

Vanna White

❀❀❀

I think I'm a better mom because my work makes me happy.

Anne Vaaler

❀❀❀

I remember it not being easy for her. But she knew she had us (Halle and her sister Heidi) and we were everything to her. So she sacrificed and she worked hard, and she made it through. It's fun to turn around and do nice things for her.

Halle Berry

❀❀❀

My mom raised me while she worked outside of
the home. This instilled in me a strong work
ethic.

Tipper Gore

❖❖❖

People see that you're no less effective because
you're a mother. You become more focused and
efficient with your time. You have to.

Gale Anne Hurd

❖❖❖

I often think back to my childhood with four sib-
lings, and wonder: How did my mother ever
manage to bring such amazing order to our hectic lives? She made it a top priority.

Jeanne Brooks-Gunn, Ph.D.

❖❖❖

I was very sick as a child, and none of the doctors could figure out what was wrong with me. But Mom was persistent. She did research at a medical-school library and found a doctor who cured me. Then, Mom herself went to medical school at age thirty-nine. Today she has her own private practice and specializes in treating people with chronic medical problems.

Michelle Block

❋ ❋ ❋

One thing I learned from my mom . . . is that you do whatever you have to for your kids.

Mary Ann Block

❋ ❋ ❋

I have a strong maternal instinct. I treat my business as if I were its mother. I treat the people I work with as a mother would.

Donna Karan

Sometimes people ask if I feel competitive with my children. Heavens, no! My big hope is that I'll be supported in my declining years!

Mary Higgins Clark

❀ ❀ ❀

If being a police officer is good enough for you, why isn't it good enough for me?

Officer Jennifer Brown,
to her mother, Officer Jo Ann Jansen

❀ ❀ ❀

As a mother of seven, grandmother of nine and a waitress for more than twenty years, my mom's had her share of sore feet. So I occasionally treat her to a foot massage. To make it extra special, I use Peppermint Foot Lotion . . .

Dorothy McFeely

❀ ❀ ❀

Humor

Dear Mom,

Thanks so much for the fun weekend at the
beach! It was great rapping with you, I mean
"exploring the goddesses within us."

I never knew you had so many boyfriends
before Daddy, but of course you made the right
choice— or what would I look like?

I've been trying to understand how you could
be so goofy about Paul Newman, and I know
you can't believe I think Tom Cruise is hot.
Maybe you raised me wrong. (Just kidding).

Anyway, you look young and fabulous, even
though you're my Mom. Gypsy Rose Lee once
said, "I have everything I had 20 years ago,
only it's all a bit lower." But that doesn't apply
to you. You're my ideal in so many "weighs,"
I mean "ways."

I love you, momfriend,
Nicole

Most kids would rather have their mothers on the brink of suicide in the next room than happy anywhere else.

Nora Ephron

◦◦◦

Surrendering to motherhood means surrendering to interruption.

Erica Jong

◦◦◦

My child looked at me and I looked back at him in the delivery room, and I realized that out of a sea of infinite possibilities it had come down to this: a specific person, born on the hottest day of the year, conceived on a Christmas Eve, made by his father and me miraculously from scratch.

Anna Quindlen

◦◦◦

48

No matter how old a mother is, she watches her middle-aged children for signs of improvement.

Florida Scott-Maxwell

⊙ ⊙ ⊙

[My mother] was passing a kidney stone and was in such atrocious pain that she could barely walk. But just before we reached the door she turned to me and, suddenly finding some new source of strength, said, "Don't forget–there's a whole chicken in the refrigerator."

Marcelle Clements

⊙ ⊙ ⊙

Ask your child what he wants for dinner only if he's buying.

Fran Lebowitz

If there were no schools to take the children away from home part of the time, the insane asylum would be filled with mothers.

Edgar Watson Howe

❀❀❀

Every person needs recognition. It is expressed cogently by the child who says, "Mother, let's play darts. I'll throw the darts and you say 'wonderful.' "

M. Dale Baugham

❀❀❀

My husband and I are either going to buy a dog or have a child. We can't decide whether to ruin our carpet or ruin our lives.

Rita Rudner

❀❀❀

Call my dad, my mom's too busy.

Chelsea Clinton,
who needed permission to get aspirin,
to her school nurse

⊙ ⊙ ⊙

Having children is like having a bowling alley installed in your brain.

Martin Mull

⊙ ⊙ ⊙

With any child . . . one hunts for the smallest indication that the child's problems will never be important enough for a television movie.

Delia Ephron

⊙ ⊙ ⊙

If you have never been hated by your child, you have never been a parent.

Bette Davis

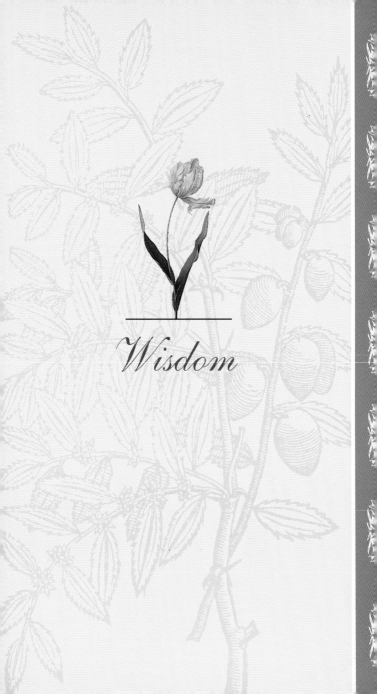

Wisdom

Dear Mom,

This letter is much overdue, but at last I think I'm mature enough to write it. Remember all the times I said to you: "That's not what I'm going to do when I have children of my own!"? Well, I know I couldn't say this face-to-face, but I want to confess that (most of the time, anyway!) you knew what you were doing.

The rules that you made, and made me follow, seemed overprotective to me, and I thought you were being a tyrant. Now I find myself making rules for my own children, and in spirit they're not that different from yours. What I think of now as gentle guidance seemed to me, as a child, more dictatorial. Today, I see the reasons behind what I saw then as a way to control me, and I'm grateful for your love and safekeeping. Thank you for having the wisdom to see me through my rebellion.

They say that history repeats itself. Maybe it'll skip a generation, and my kids will be more like you than like me. I hope so!

Your grateful daughter,
Grace

I want him to learn to be responsible for his own actions. And to try not to be judgmental. Just kind of lay back and give people the benefit of the doubt. I want him to be loving and compassionate.

Meg Ryan

◌ ◌ ◌

My mother continually influences my relationship with my daughter. My mother has taught me how to raise my daughter, to look at Anna as a unique person and not make her into something I want her to be, but to guide her on a path—not take her off her path and put her on mine.

Elyse Shapiro

◌ ◌ ◌

My ultimate goal always was to have a family. Now that's come true. Now my goal is to teach my children how to grow up with love and discipline.

Vanna White

○ ○ ○

Kids have a way of bringing purity back to life. That's what's important. To raise children. Decent human beings.

Whitney Houston

○ ○ ○

An ounce of mother is worth a ton of priest.

Spanish Proverb

○ ○ ○

After all, if you bungle bringing up your children, it doesn't really matter what you do with the rest of your life.

Sigourney Weaver

My mother was always on me to be neat and pick up after myself. Those lessons taught me how to be responsible.

Kim Alexis

◦◦◦

Failure to know your mother, that is, your position and its attendant traditions, history and place in the scheme of things, is failure to remember your significance, your reality, your right relationship to earth and society. It is the same as being lost—isolated, abandoned, self-estranged, and alienated from your own life.

Paula Gunn Allen

◦◦◦

You want to make the most of every little scrap life gives you. My mother taught me that.

Joyce Maynard

◦◦◦

Smart mothers know that tantrums and cross words will, from time to time, cloud the sunny experiences we want for our children. So when nerves get frazzled, these mothers step back, take a breather and bank on the most important yet simplest guidelines of all: Just love them.

Sue Woodman

◦◦◦

My mother never lectured. She had no conscious philosophy of life or childraising. But her attitude and beliefs were so consistent, so strongly expressed in action, that I followed as if reproducing the steps of a dance. I learned from my mother not to be idle. There is always *something* to do—the ideal being two things at once. When Mother cleaned house, she wrapped old towels around her shoes: a little extra footwork polished the floors.

Fredelle Maynard

◦◦◦

In an old song the Mother sings: "My sleeping is my dreaming, my dreaming is my thinking, my thinking is my wisdom." She is the bed we are born in, in which we sleep and dream, where we are healed, love and die. In her wisdom we remember day's broken images and carry them down into dreams where their motions roll into shadows and root, growing into stories.

Meinrad Craighead

✧ ✧ ✧

I do believe I am a good mother. I try to stay out of my children's way. I try to give them information because I worry, but you can't figure out all their problems for them. You can only assist.

Debbie Reynolds

✧ ✧ ✧

For me, woman is not fulfilled unless she's a mother.

Sophia Loren

Being a mother means that I must be available to my children, not all the time, mind you, but enough so they know I am receptive to whatever they have to share. This is the basis of good communication.

Beth Shannon

✿✿✿

My mother was my first, best teacher.

Fredelle Maynard

✿✿✿

I get like a tigress when it's about my kids.

Meryl Streep

✿✿✿

I am framing and displaying this portrait I love because it is through my young daughter's eyes that I see I have become a woman I never thought I could become.

Kathryn Harrison

My mother was a firm ruler. If there were any obstacles in the way she would ignore them. If any unwelcome facts upset her hopes, she would treat them as if they didn't exist.

Christopher Milne

◇ ◇ ◇

You give up your self, and finally you don't even mind. I wouldn't have missed this for anything. It humbled my ego and stretched my soul. It gave me whatever crumbs of wisdom I possess today.

Erica Jong

◇ ◇ ◇

I used to try to shape my family in the image of the family I grew up in. But my mom helped me see things differently. She told me, "You have to create your own family. You have to come up with a new model that works for you."

Ann Vaaler

I had an extraordinary mother. . . . She was
funny and dear and outrageous. She was
demanding, entertaining, joyful, curious, original, maddening, overwhelming, brave, hard-
working, deeply flawed, and, above all, profoundly lovable. I am a mother myself, so why
did it take me 35 years to understand that mothers aren't perfect?

Joyce Maynard

◦◦◦

She gives me good advice all the time. Her
instincts are so incredible.

Swoosie Kurtz

◦◦◦

And maybe it's time we admitted that a lot of the
traits—good and bad—we blame on Mom would
be better attributed to life.

Sara Nelson